La Gioconda

Tony Nesca

<u>By Tony Nesca</u>

Stale Anchovy Kisses -

Dead Bats Amidst The Bullshit Laughter And The Lovestricken Cockroaches –

Hollow Man –

La Gioconda -

Charlie -

Mondo Cane -

Dishpig -

About A Girl -

Emma Strunk -

Jukebox Music -

La Gioconda (the novel) -

The Do-Nothing Boys -

Bulletproof Smile -

Vodka Orange Sunday -

Hobo –

Crazy Legs –

Junkyard Lucy -

ISBN: **978-1-7752112-2-8**

Published by Screamin' Skull Press

screamingskullpress.net/

Printed in the U.S.A.

Things always seem to end before they start

Lou Reed

An artist is somebody who enters into competition with

God.

Patti Smith

What you are about to read is a work of fiction

La Gioconda

1.

It was in the wake of a tragedy, the kind that tears your brains out all things looking ugly, the kind that leaves you eyes vacant limp body on pavement, mind gone wiry, toothless hag in your underwear, barroom whispers constant companion, sipping whiskey in dark corners, dark mind wanting soft morning breeze, god distant enemy, nightmare visions daytime wandering, people ugly and vicious, sidewalk woman long cool hateful transparent in the morning haze you live breathe shit drink in confusion mind-state, 'nother rye I tells him, 'nother soft restraint if you please, sympathy for endless night, sun ugly and cold, dancing at the end of the world it was in the wake of this kind of tragedy that I met Jasmina...

Started drinking at age 15 been one party-drunk after another somehow ending up at a particular dark downtown drinking hole called The Brass Rail facing

the tragedy head-on drinking Rye and 7 shooting the
shit with bartender large scarred face black tie curly
blond hair and red-faced, commotion in corner tough
guys arguing insults turned to fists, bartender hopped
bar joined the sadness, I drank drank talking to hooker
beside me, she was sweet low-down slight black eye
pouty lips, black fellow with dreads showed up from
nowhere and shook my hand,

 "You alright" he said "you alright" Fucker kept
moving past gang members bandanas wrapped around
their heads tough talk in the loud music hip-hop coming
from juke, red carpet covered in cig butts hooker smiled
sadly it's alright I told her, alright,

 "Yeah?" she said quietly "you sure?"

I said nothing ordered more juice man, old drunk sat
alone hair gone wild front tooth missing he spat on floor
laughing, I moved towards the washroom smelling the
piss approaching damn filthy reality toilet plugged bugs
crawling the floor, got unzipped started laughing for a
few seconds then fell silent...some very strange things
had led me up to that precise moment, some karmic
displeasure hanging around my life as electricity shot
across the room and right through me shake rattle rock
and roll loser, young native guy in mirror behind bar
started coughing up a lung almost fell off his chair kept

going for long time as I asked bartender for a shot of
sambuca, cough cough behind me, sure he said, on the
house, cough cough arggg, pretty nice day I said to
bartender, cough, jesus, argg cough cough, sure he said,
nice day, guy in mirror struggling to get it out coughing
so fucking hard it was almost noiseless then it started
again, fucking hell awarrrgg cough shit shit cough,
bartender staring wild-eyed crazy,

"Jesus hell" said hooker with black eye "you gonna live
or what?"

"No, cough cough, problem" said native guy, gave one
last thunderous outburst then stopped dead...

"I'll have a rye and coke" he said lighting cigarette and
continuing, smiling, spittle on cheek scratching his balls
uggg he said, gruaghg, big fucking black guys always
hung around the pool table looking tough man, no
trouble in that part of bar with the gold chains and the
black leather one guy long scar on forehead murder in
his eyes, I had no problem with that place felt almost at
home with the rummies and gang fuckheads never
forgetting that I was a tourist, it wasn't where I was
from, it was a temporary exploration, I figured, I hoped,
large familiar lady from downtown scene came through
back door drunk and stoned sat beside me talking shit,

"You know you want it boy" she said "I can see your cock pushing at your jeans, I can lick it from top to bottom, you know, I'm good at it, just say the word boy"

"Not today, thanks, anything else?"

"What do you mean?"

"Anything else on your mind?"

"What the fuck else is there?"

"What else is there? Are you fucking serious?"

"Don't want to talk to you no more"

"Fuck off then"

She moved away scowling hurt in her eyes me feeling bad as hell for being such a prick but fuck it, don't see many people considering my feelings few more rye's down the throat inane conversation with bartender then slowly made my way out back door late March cool breeze sun just beginning to go down on Ellice Avenue and the core area flunkies man, small patches of snow lingered on boulevard I smoked in the crisp night blowing clouds into the air feeling alone and alright depressed and alright reached Portage Avenue downtown couple of drunks passed out in bus shack guy down the street screaming at the top of his lungs making strange sounds echoing through the downtown sad, freaky fucking city I stood at bus stop waiting for goddamn bus to take me out of the relentless drunken assault of the core area bored and restless lighting a joint inhaling deeply, the fuck with it, felt the sadness on me like a second skin eyes filling up with tears I fought it off taking it all in, every last bit of it…

2.

Middle of the day still sleeping phone ringing incessantly hangover hovering around the edges, I let the answering machine do the work heard a distant familiar voice,

"Tony, it's Trent, you there?...haven't seen you at school for awhile man, what's going on?...listen, I'm sitting here with two gorgeous chicks and-"

"-Hello…"

"Tony, what the fuck?"

"I was crashed man…what's up?"

"Well, got two chicks here, one is an exchange student from France, she's staying with my parents in Gimli, the other…"

"-Yeah?"

"Got a bottle of Crown Royal and some beer, wanna come over? I'll come get you in ten minutes"

Silence…

"Tony…"

"Yeah, alright, give me twenty minutes or so, uhh…"

"See ya then"…

Walked into Trent's apartment feeling alright things considered, two young women at a table bottle of rye between them both looking good and meaty, one very short, other tall as hell, both dressed in black didn't really give a fuck about either of them but good looking broads all around can be good for the spirit, sat down at table Trent pouring the rye conversation alright both girls in high school but not typical bullshit pretty intelligent especially short one talking about writers, Huxley, A. Munroe, Mordecai Richler, Henry Miller, tall one cutting in with that beautiful French accent mentioning Bukowski and Anais Nin and Knut Hamsun, started having a good time all things ugly moving to back of brain Trent telling me about philosophy paper he's doing on Kierkegaard, c'mon man I said, that's bullshit talk, alright alright he laughed, smart guy that Trent and intellectual talk WAS my thing but recent events turned mind elsewhere so the talking continued,

"So where you been man?" Said Trent

"Just hanging out alone, you know, different places"

"Those places you're hanging out at can kill you, you know that?"

"I've hung out there off and on for years, it's no problem"

"People get shanked at The Brass Rail all the time man"

"It's not a problem, I'm telling you"

"Lots of places like that in France" said the French girl thick accent "they don't scare me either"

I cheered her lit a smoke started talking about some of the shit I've seen down there in the demilitarized zone bums everywhere begging for pennies people getting busted up in back alleys over nothing but a case of beer no fucking work no love all anger little hope everyone drinking getting high getting laid the good things in life, they laugh laugh laugh touch of sadness, hah hah hah, people starving in those places but what the hell, laughter always a good thing, Trent sort of morose type but capable of the good talk, the good laughter when mood was right so we laughed and drank REM blasting in the background then The Replacements, Midnight Oil, The Jam, started lighting the joints passing them around that powerful hydroponic shit making us all see things differently collective unconscious expanding, as Huxley suggested, our brains are hard-wired for this...short girl called Karla talked to me intently steady-line, steady- focus, I was digging this young high school beauty just turned 18, how old are you she said,

"Twenty-seven"

"You go to school with Trent?"

"Yeah, third year University, not very interesting at all"

"What are you taking?"

"Psychology courses mainly, they're alright, the rest can kiss my ass"

"I like you"

"I see"

French girl just sat on the outside interjecting the occasional laugh or comment in that crazy accent all of us having a blast night coming reality twisted feeling the sadness breathing down my neck fought it back relentless motherfucker hanging around the edges always blue light at end of dark hallway madness suicide wanting, started talking fast waving my hands while everyone listened intensely in groove with my strange-way thinking Trent laughed and laughed then took over with some of his tales and bizarre observations, odd kid, gotta-love-it French chick in own world drew her knees up, glimpse of skin between the socks and the pant-leg olive colored beauty found myself wondering what her thighs looked like big meaty bouncy, Karla talking with me, to me, she was a fireball man, energy coming out of her thunder-light waterfall liked her right off the bat thought maybe I could end up with her ass cheeks on my lips uh-huh, we were getting high and drunk all of us young stupid and invulnerable, in that state anything could happen, took a glance at the French girl, she seemed to look superior withdrawn...bitch I thought, let's go out I howled, let's fuck things up good and proper, Trent took a long look at Karla's tits and suggested The Tom-Tom Club, alright we screamed on the edge of nothing superior thinking mind-waste we got into Trent's car as he started the engine too drunk to drive, too drunk to care...

3.

Tom-Tom Club in the Osborne Village freaky part of town sort of tiny Greenwich Village we was sitting around in this wild place everyone dressed in black white faces black lipstick army boots downing rye and 7 shots of sambuca man Frenchie beside me loud alternative band cranking out the rock-punk,

"So what's your name?" I said

"WHAT? CAN'T HEAR YOU, MUSIC'S TOO LOUD"

"WHAT'S YOUR NAME?"

"JASMINA...LET'S DANCE"

Dragged me to dance floor slam dancing into the bodies rubbing against us fierce eyes saying something, Karla started whole thing insane stage diving into sea of drunken corpses hands on her tits and ass rolling right by my head me reaching out trying to cop a feel, got tired of that shit moved back to table convinced dancing is for morons, Jasmina downed her drink raised empty glass at me, I ordered another for her and me we hit glasses the hell with it, Trent having a ball John Lennon glasses long curly hair thinning up top he was laughing drinking drinking to the end of the long silent night cuz it don't mean shit anyway, he waved me over to dark corner,

"LISTEN MAN, I…UH…YOU KNOW, WHAT YOU AND YOUR FAMILY JUST WENT THROUGH…I MEAN…I DON'T WANT YOU TO THINK I ABANDONED YOU, YOU KNOW?...THESE KINDS OF THINGS ARE TRICKY…"

"DON'T MENTION IT MAN" placed a hand on his shoulder "YOU'RE A GOOD FRIEND"

"WHAT?"

"YOU'RE…NO PROBLEM, LET'S GO"

"SAY AGAIN…"

I made a motion back to our table shaking his hand he was digging it, we were caught in the moment a little loving baby shake it all around up and over reality train impossible, Jasmina and Karla on dance floor alone gyrating hips legs gone wiry man, breasts juggling strobe lights on scanning the crowd of Osborne Village freaks got goth couple in corner pretending to be somber, bartender large fellow big black beard grinning bastard, group of punkers on second level hung out chugging beer with DOA stickers on their jackets, young girl with pierced nose lip eyebrows at table beside us swaying to the music, bartender starts moving like caged animal stroking his beard dark and lonely, Jasmina's ass high up in the air Karla looking small and nasty and sexual animal man, they slow moving gyro, they liquid-metal up and down easy street, they groovin' punk rock violence, tall lanky fellow eyeing Jasmina's brazilian ass as it tilted one way then the other, he hypnotized man, he lost in sex-hungry maybees, all of us lost permanently in life gone haywire, purple haze gone John and Ringo dead and buried George hanging with Jimi even Sid Vicious sad and beautiful leather jacket creaking in the wind old man drowning in filthy pool out back at the end of the universe, me thinking Johnny was, yeah, Johnny was something unlike anything, got couple of goth girls on dance floor one tall and blond long tattered dress purple shirt, other pitch black from head to toe torn fishnets, they standing there drinks in hand slightly, ever so slightly moving to the music be-bop, a distant hazy reality started thinking about the tall one's thighs picturing them in all possible positions, all possible sixes and shapes, pictured them wrapped tightly around my head face turning purple ecstatic frenzy man, tall guy talking Jasmina up on dance floor I see her pointing at me I give the guy the peace sign, Trent laughing in background drinking madly, no fear, no tomorrow, no god, nothing happening but right here right now, short bald guy soliciting me with drugs strobe lights pumping it up almost violent all okay by the whorehouse on the corner lit up like a fireball, I inhaled marijuana right there and then in the days when you could do that, days gone in the tornado confusion butt-ugly politician making everything ugly freedom out the window la la la, well well, I suppose a beautiful sad sight all around world rotating just out of synch Trent and I looking at each other smiling till the blues walked through the door and circled the room and I started thinking too much about useless things better forgotten tragedy coming to forefront I shook Trent's hand downed my drink walking out the door outside nice and cool crisp air in my lungs, sidewalk full of fringe-living midnight-people with their own problems and tragedies no one gets out alive man, no way…

$$4.$$

Was staying at my mother's house at the time she in Italy with husband leaving me with big house nice neighborhood tall trees lining the streets forming a canopy over the hot summer sidewalks, had small bed in basement large stereo back yard six foot fence affording the privacy I needed sitting there on a small bench under thick tree cutting classes drinking wine hangover afternoon in early spring cool, house on corner of busy street could hear traffic running wild but saw nothing 'cept for green leaves and grass felt excluded from all things people looking ugly to me but working on getting out of the deep blue soul-sucker moment, heard lawn mower in distance, a dog barked, car horns someone swearing, poor fuckers, sadness of human existence everywhere you look pour a glass of wine and forget it man, went inside came back out with my guitar had another hit of wine and a toot began to play the sad-mourning crawling away from me just a little...

5.

Few weeks went by University dead and ugly spent most time at downtown watering holes small table by window, always some fucked-up young chick talking all kinds of shit, or some poor bastard confessing his latest sins spewing out the inevitable arm in arm dancing through the lost landscape, any meaning in all this lost to me walking down Ellice Avenue with the rest of the spent-world-gone-wrong, dim-light-glory blue murder distant meaning, ending up back at Trent's playing poker with scotch and soda cigarettes and some red-hair sensi, doing alright now is what I kept saying still capable of good time not completely destroyed, never completely, it's all alright you fucking punk lay down the hand win few bucks crooked smile telling me things ain't over, not by a long shot – never completely – knock at the door Jasmina walked in black leather jacket blue-jeans hair slicked back in a bun, very nice how quaint, god you're just simply put too damn beautiful is what I was thinking, man oh man, Trent doing his thing began talking philosophy let's do it man he said let's do it! Guy alright wild cynic too fucking self-involved for clarity Billie Holliday in background Jasmina talking much very engaging young woman,

"Well I'm in town for another week" She said

"Good stuff" I said

"You alright?"

"Couldn't be better"

"Got some French wine, you, ahh"

"Well, uh, don't know.."

Doorbell rang again Trent running around insane depressed invulnerable laughing manic opens door old friend named Jake long sideburns hair like young Tony Curtis shy grin stoned eyes immediately on Jasmina,

"Hello" He said "You know, someone once said that dogs fuck the pope and maybe…"

"Hi" She smiled wide and large and sad,

"Tony you hound-dog"

"What you want man?" I said,

"Drinking again, ey?"

"What else my man, what the hell else?"

We shook hands old friend's eyes knowing, Satchmo in background playing sad trumpet low-down-mood is alright,

"Here men" Jasmina sarcastic laughter "Someone open this wine"

Jake moved quickly bottle in hand corkscrew stuck way too deep, damn thing, sliver of cork came out rest stayed in bottle,

"Well, look, I…" Said Jake,

"Thank you" Jasmina winking pushed cork inside took very long pull of wine I watched the liquid slide down the bottle into her throat saw her ass sticking upwards, she paused, then a short sip bottle down wet lips dribble of wine lit a smoke just like that man not on stage, not giving a shit whether anyone saw it or not, moving natural motion man easy cool, bit clumsy, her eyes on mine I poured the Scotch felt something in the night feeling right and wrong distant beauty dark lights in my head…

Trent and Jasmina played poker in kitchen Jake chewed my ear off in living room by small balcony looking out at upscale neighborhood,

"…for the duration of the class man"

"For that long?" I said,

"Yeah, no bullshit!"

"Well what the fuck, did you do something?"

"I went up to her and started talking about the Blue Rodeo concert, that one we went to at the University"

"Smooth"

"She fucking shot me down man"

"Really?"

"Without saying a word, not a word, her fucking glance was enough to slaughter an army of assholes like me, you know?"

We started laughing,

"Who gives a shit, women, who the fuck are they?"

"Who are they, that's right!"

He looked over at Trent and Jasmina she was laughing slamming down cards delicate and foreign, Trent grim and loosing,

"Man, that Jasmina…" Said Jake,

"Yep"

"I've got problems with my asshole" He said,

"At the outer rim or internal?"

"Uhhh…a little of both, I think"

"I see."

The Hoodoo Gurus were on in the background and I was digging it looking around the plush condo with sunken living-room, wall to wall carpet, state of the art computer, Woody Allen posters, washer and drier on the premises, dining room, living room, encyclopedias, dictionaries, 3 bedrooms, 2 bathrooms, a balcony facing an upscale part of town with identical houses lined up neatly like convicts on death row, all paid for by the parents as long as the kids did their thing at school, similar arrangement to what I had but my neighborhood not so nice and who gives a shit anyway? So Trent started talking about some greek philosopher that did this or that boring the shit out of everyone Jasmina trying to look interested cuz she was that kind of gal Jake he wondering and cruising in his own mind full of insecurities and tough grace, I focused on his Tony Curtis hair for awhile feeling jealous and awkward then announced I was going for a walk reaching for the bottle of Rye,

 "I'll come too" Said Jasmina,
Jake said something crazy but I wasn't listening and we were off…

6.

We walked through a complex of condos laid out like a maze surrounded by small lakes and grass last remnants of snow still spotting the landscape everything Canadian-cool-winter-spring, everything silent slice of moon up above, car engine somewhere in the far off distance, a door slammed shut, crickets making me real nervous man saw a duck skim one of the lakes Jasmina putting the bottle to her lips letting it flow, she had a clumsy walk leaning forward like she could fall at any second which made her that much more beautiful of course as the silence continued at the end of all things...then she spoke...

"You're kinda short" She said,

"I see."

"How tall are you?"

"Somewhere around 5'8"...you must be about 5'10""

"Somewhere around there...you know, I'm going to Texas tomorrow."

"Why the hell would anyone go to Texas?"

"My grandmother lives there."

"I thought you said you were in town for another weekend?"

"I lied"

"How do you afford all these trips man?"

"It's all part of that stupid student exchange program, they pay for everything."

"What a tough life."

"I don't see you suffering."

"Hey, I've got a place to live thanks to family, if it wasn't for them I'd be out on the street…"

"What's family for, right?"

I put the bottle on my lips letting it go like thunder,

"Yeah, what are they for…" I said,

"You know, I really like it here"

"Here, in this neighborhood?"

"No, I can do without this…"

She almost tripped both of us laughing and feeling it, feeling the moment soon to be gone,

"I mean here in Canada, it's refreshing"

"Yeah, I kinda dig it myself"

"Where else have you been except for here?"

"Well, I was born in Italy, did junior high school there, seen several Italian cities, few Canadian cities, been to Minneapolis to see The Stones….that's about it, don't give a damn about traveling"

"I know what you mean, I've traveled a lot because my parents pushed it on me, you know that liberal

European thinking, see the world, all that, personally I don't give a shit…do you know?"

"I know, I know"

"Gimli is very beautiful, don't you know?"

"I've heard…how old are you?"

"18…why?"

"Just wondering…you look young"

"Don't you love it?" She laughed man, she just laughed out of the blue like the whole fucking thing means some powerful cosmic shit,

"And you?"

"27"

"When I get back from Texas I'd like to spend more time in Winnipeg, what do you think?"

"I think, I think"

"What's wrong with you?"

"Hey, kitty-kat, who's your favorite band?"

"The Cure"

"That doesn't count"

"What? Why?"

"The Cure is not a band"

"What the fuck?"

"They are a sad sad imitation of one"

We both laughed she chasing me through the late-night fog 'round the lakes and hills and suburban deathly-quiet,

"What about you mister superman, who's your favorite band?" She said as we stopped full-stop-baby catching our breaths thinking wild songs in the moonlight,

"The Pixies, who else?"

"Great band…listen, too much fucking money in this neighborhood…let's go back"

"I thought you were a rich girl?"

"I am…but I don't like it, and wipe that smile off your face"

I started running again her behind me laughing clumsy pace doomed to failure,

"Where's Trent's place?" She screaming after me,

"Follow me" Running out of breath I went this way that way saw her long long legs behind me feeling damn good about it man, feeling the slow easy night cold early morning crocodile hangover looking ugly silent red and black constipated thinking clouds of lonely wanderings tiger-hunt alright blood flows crimson-red young girl on urban corner she goddamn beautiful she short-hand-sexy, she uptown lovely, she on her sad knees giving lonely answers, Jasmina I sing, Jasmina…

7.

Oldest friend Barney was back in town on leave from his Greenpeace job sailing the world having a motherfucking ball while trying to make things better esoteric conversations in the green-days ahead with wild-toxic-nothings in my ear,

"Let's go meet Jake" I said,

"Gotcha man"

He looking sad, off his rhythm, long black ponytail halfway down his back speckled with grey same as the beard 6' 3" Canadian Indian we was walking through the Osborne Village cool summer day he telling me about his lady dumping him for another guy, this being one of the toughest things to take in life, nothing worse short of death, yours or someone else's, myself having been there more than once not liking that damn alone-feeling man, that lost-look-feeling following the midnight hour,

"You know, I'm never lonely Barney, never! Except for right after I've been dumped..."

"That last time stayed with you man, remember?...that's what I'm going through right now, this time it was big, you know?...we made all sorts of plans, I can't fucking believe I was making plans, ME, can you believe it?"

"I've come to the conclusion that a relationship, the romantic kind, should be viewed as an added attraction in life, not the main show"

"Huh, maybe you're right, I don't know…."

"It's a social construct, that's all…you really think we're meant to be with one lifelong monogamous mate?…I don't buy it for one fucking second"

"What then?"

"I don't know, maybe we're supposed to have several different relationships through our life, each of varying lengths and meaning, you know?"

"I don't think anything's 'meant' or 'supposed' to be, when you say shit like that you're implying divine order, that's a whole other can of worms"

"I meant in the biological sense, we're inclined to do certain things"

"Yeah, but there's more than biology and science, we've discussed this before, remember?"

"I do…maybe there's more, maybe there isn't…what other conclusion can you draw?"

"Listen, not to change the subject, but to change it completely, I wish I could have been with you for that shit that went down with your family…that's tough man, how you making out?"

"Just peachy man, just peachy"

We sat for a second in silence surrounded by squeegee kids with tall beautiful Mohawks smell of marijuana in the air on the corner of Stradbrook Street and Osborne starving artists university students with their pointed shoes and spiky hair we was playing the slow lament tune wind whistling Dixieland blues, firetruck making its run old drunk walked out of sleazy hotel he stumbling poor desperate poor, punk rocker hand stretched out I gave him his bread man Barney adding a few coins we was hillbilly intellectual riding the death-ship unafraid bloody and cornered,

"Let's forget about it" I said,

"I hear ya, there's The Toad In The Hole, is it open yet, let's have a dozen"

The Toad was an Irish pub I think Jake already there taking in the fumes could hear Louis Armstrong in the background Jake sitting in a corner by a window facing the Osborne Village with all the freaks parading their shit up and down the street while Satchmo played the blues, sorta dark place emblems from U.K. soccer teams all over the walls fish and chips kidney pie young people hanging out at the tables old guys at the bar, not kidding when I say Jake could have fit in to the early jazz era perfectly with that thin mustache cigarette dangling from his lips man insecure sneer hair thick as the devil's, Barney ran to him they hugging while the music switched to Celtic room thick with smoke, we talked at light speed all at the same time words rolling off our tongues like spider-web fantasies, good friends listen closely while piano plays solo at the midnight serenade, cool cool movement running down Bourbon Street, love that clarinet she plays as I pack my suitcase Jack greengrass telling me shit doodle dandy, got the blues mama he tells her street corner hooker laughing in the rain, "you like jazz?" she saying "you like blues?" as I dance through the grim sunlight church bell ringing, feeling easy street under my shoes jazz-man old and wiry smiles crocodile beer and crucifix wine,

"…christ man (in mid-conversation), you're like Indiana-fucking-Jones" Said Jake,

"Seen the world twice over" Said Barney,

"But do you really think you guys are accomplishing anything?"

Music plays on feel Bessie Smith eyeballing me crotch heavy with sensation, two lesbians making love-electric, love-electric tornado valley brimming sexual movement that girl shaking her THING to that fucking crazy Ska beat ass rotating Wildman-blues, she slinks over red red lips wide open long moody thigh slips in and out of black dress, "what's up baby?" she says old drunk leaning forward gives a wink and a smile "what's up love-thing juicy?",

  "Look Jake, it's not really about whether we're actually stopping anything.."

  "Well then what the fuck…"

  "Let me finish…it's about raising awareness to an issue so that the people with the real power will fucking do something"

  "You guys are both talking shit" I said,

  Walking the sweaty Winnipeg summer streets man see the long-distance-runner copping a feel, see that old crazy broad on the corner giving head in rhythm bop bop bang, she got one tooth missing she beautiful and distant, hear the muted horn as it sings that sad note early Sunday morning, can you hear it? off-key love all there is, she banging those round wild hips all over the world, she got sleepy overbite mouth closing over it like rose pedal madness, you gotta see Paris in the moonlight she says, don't give a damn about Paris I say her ass in my face telling me stories, touch her lips with mine softly explode while running the gauntlet,

"All I'm saying" Said Jake "Is that I can't stand futile efforts that are really, really, just an attempt to appease your own conscience...it's like someone saying, 'I will not buy any stolen car stereos, that's my part'...what the fuck does that do?...is that going to stop the theft of car stereos?...of course fucking not...this is futile bullshit that solves nothing"

"You couldn't be more wrong man, think what would happen if by setting the example more people, a lot of people, maybe even most people, would stop buying stolen car stereos?..do you see what I mean?"

"He's got you there" I said ordering a few shots of Sambuca,

Waitress 5 foot tall big hips and tits like the atom bomb brown eyes large beautiful round thighs genuine smile 18 or 19 years old T-shirt says 'hug me', who wants anything more I think, who deserves anything more keep the music going she fall down lovely she got it electrifying old man trouble we in love I say, oh yeah she says we cooked in lust cuz you know it don't mean a thing if it ain't got that yeah-yeah,

"I think both of you got it wrong" I said, "you're missing the bigger picture"

"Oh yeah?" Said Barney,

"Yeah, all anyone has to do in life, their only obligation, is to live in character, to do exactly what comes naturally to them, know what I mean?...when you live OUT of character, that's when depression sets in and the whole world goes out of whack"

Night always comes from a distance purple and grey, out in the graveyard the devil sings in the moody dusk he got the midnight blues guitar out of tune wails forever, forever lonely and beautiful she winks like madness, she smiles happy discord silent wisp in your ear goes nuclear baby baby baby please don't go,

"Besides the fact that I get chicks from all over the world" Said Barney,

"You got me there man" Said Jake shaking Barney's hand,

"Yum yum googly-fuck" I said,

"Tell him about Jasmina" Said Jake

"This tall French chick Barney, goddamn almost indescribable beauty man, sexy sexy, 18 years old"

"That's a bit young, wouldn't you say?"

"Normally I would agree with you but she's different, very intelligent and mature, and experienced...it's different in Europe, you know?"

"More mature than you" Said Jake wiry grin,

"Sounds funky" Said Barney,

"I'll bet" I interrupted those fuckers "as soon as she sees you, Barney, she'll make a B-line straight for you"

"I wouldn't mind meeting her"

Then his head went down for an instant thinking about someone else, someplace else, she crawls into your mind nothing you can do pal, brain tilts to one side and slips out your ear tough-looking wise guy butts cigarette on the face of the world gone far far insane, slinking down that filthy back alley with the garbage cans like tombstones she winks goodbye, goodbye cuz the sky's blue and lonely, goodbye cuz the punk-rock jazz beat can't last forever, goodbye cuz there ain't nothing else to do in a smoke-filled room but keep singing honest lies about love and hate as the sky turns red/purple and dances fat-ass wanting to the end of the night...

8.

About one hour into our drinking discussion Trent walked in Jasmina right behind him a full head taller tight jeans black leather jacket hair greased back and tied tightly in a bun, Trent had the John Lennon glasses faded jean-jacket he looking hippie-suave with that punk-edge looking at Barney with distrust them two never liking each other but shaking hands anyway phony bastards I loved them both as I look through bloodshot ever-curious eyeballs seeing world-gone mad mad mad, introduced Barney and Jasmina she looking like the word beauty invented just for her barney's eyeballs shooting straight across the fucking room, "let's go to the Spectrum" I howled, "to the fucking Spectrum, my children!"

9.

The Spectrum was Canada's premier alternative rock bar, it was sweet and lowdown, it was low-ride-crazy man, every night great live music bombarded your central nervous system with messages of sex rebellion dark-mind-wasted your senses shake rattle and rolling all over the dance floor baby, young University crowd wanting more always more and more grinding body against body all serious shit forgotten cuz it's sun-go-down gymnastics now, got no time for scholastic bullshit twist and shout that rock and roll ass sweet sixteen gone crazy…mostly alternative rock, ska and punk but saw every musical style there, young crowd, smart crowd, tough crowd it was all there man as we stood against the front bar few feet from the stage, me in front leaning with elbow against bar digging the ska band cranking out the rhythm my leg moving forward, then back, then slightly to the left, Jasmina hanging over my shoulder never too far, never too far round Brazilian ass pointing upwards like a soccer ball, I would hang at the back and there she was big smile telling me something, move over to other side of bar and there she was again moving to the rhythm red lips wide and happy, huuuummm I started thinking what the hell, Barney dancing with young women Trent observing all laughing laughing he runnin' with the devil man, whole room swinging to the Friday night beat, the hell with the world and all the lost causes,

"Hey" tap on my shoulder, Barney there breathing heavy "looks like she made a b-line for the wrong guy"

"What? Can't hear you?"

"LOOKS LIKE SHE MADE A B-LINE FOR THE WRONG GUY"

"WHO?"

"THE FRENCH CHICK, WHAT'S HER NAME?"

"JASMINA…YEAH, I'M STARTING TO NOTICE"

"FUCK THIS UP AND I'LL KILL YOU, JUST OUT OF PRINCIPLE MAN"

"JUICY"

"HERE SHE COMES AGAIN MAN" he started walking away backwards "LOOKOUT BABY, LIKE-WOW-WIPEOUT!"

I turned around and there she was man, face moist light touch of sweat she was smiling from ear to ear huge brown-green sad-speaking eyes leaning into me Friday night music-man kingfish joker gangster of lust sweet sweet lovers and sinners all around us…

10.

"You having a good time?" She said

"What?"

"ARE YOU HAVING A GOOD TIME?"

"Oh YEAH, YEAH, LOVE THIS PLACE...GREAT FUCKING BAND"

"YOU KNOW A LOT OF WOMEN"

"THEY'RE ALL UNIVERSITY FRIENDS...HAVEN'T BEEN HERE IN A LONG TIME, YOU KNOW..."

"BACK IN FRANCE THERE ISN'T MUCH OF THIS AT ALL"

"SAY AGAIN, I DIDN'T GET THAT"

"BACK IN FRANCE...THE CITY I LIVE IN..."

"WHAT CITY IS THAT?"

"STRASBOURG...THERE AREN'T ANY BARS LIKE THIS"

"REALLY?"

"NOTHING...JUST RAP, HIP-HOP BULLSHIT, TECHNO, SO MUCH TECHNO CRAP, IT DRIVES ME CRAZY"

"IT WOULD DRIVE ME TO SUICIDE"

Pause...we looked at each other something happening in our heads -

"YOU'RE THE MOST BEAUTIFUL WOMAN IN THIS PLACE" I said,

"IS THAT ALL YOU THINK OF ME?"

"THAT'S ALL I KNOW OF YOU"

"YOU'RE RIGHT...ARE YOU COMING TO TRENT'S AFTER THE BAR?"

"IS THAT WHAT'S GOING ON?"

"YEAH"

"THEN I JUST MIGHT..."

After that I approached the stage elbow on bar sipping on scotch and water listening to the Ska band tear it up people I know approaching, talking, laughing, and I laugh and talk and laugh cuz I'm polite not cuz I give a shit, not cuz I give a damn what happens to world gone distant hazy, world gone missing in action populated by jack-knife sensibilities, don't kid yourself man, no one gives a damn, not really...

3 in the morning all drunk and high listening to Stevie Ray Vaughn's "Texas Flood" got Woody Allen movie on with the sound off Trent and Barney had been arguing all night long driving everyone fucking crazy but eyelids getting heavy all around cept for me and Jasmina, we

singing the redemption song, we deep in the heart of the songs of the doomed, she had changed into a pair of shorts and a wool sweater calf-high white socks, her legs just how I had suspected long and well-rounded olive-skin big thighs young and powerful beside me on the couch as one by one OUR guests had fallen into drunk-sleep, Jake and Trent on the armchairs Barney on the floor, me and Jasmina on the couch large jug of wine half-empty on coffee table we were lazy wine-drunk talking cool and comfortable like old friends who had shared everything for 10,000 years, she was caressing my forearm laying side by side her tits grinding into me as REM sang the sad songs,

"Why don't you let your hair down?" I said,

"Too greasy tonight...I'll wear it down next time"

She got up me watching her thighs jiggle away and that round brazilian ass high up tilting left then right so rare on white women man yet there it was, changed the music to the Barenaked Ladies' first record, the "Brian Wilson" song, poured more wine then those thighs slid over to me like a snake and we laid down her head on my shoulder letting the words flow easy and cool and feeling that damn thing that happens so rarely between people, instant electricity jolting you back to reality, not the man-made mad-money world reality, not the cellophane wrapped bullshit society reality, not that monstrous thing you navigate day after day that ugly place where you're judged by the size of your wallet or the cost of your car or the price of your recent sell-out, but the real world of love and hate, song and dance, everything internal and fantastic and elusive beauty everywhere…

She'd be nervous talking agitated hand movements sticking her tongue out looking like a schoolgirl making excuses, then there were heavy sensual moments of serious deliberation where she stared at nothing looking waaaay beyond her 18 years reflective and mature thinking deep cooool waves of long-living illusion, blue smoke trailing from her cig curling up to the ceiling I watched her move and grind then started my own thing she watching me with same intent I talked all kind of shit man wisdom pouring out of my young veins wine glass in hand cigarette always smoking and her brown-green eyes, her brown-green eyes looking right into me I took her hand and slid the other around her waist feeling all soft flesh ripe and beautiful, she took off her socks showing me her feet, long and elegant toes un-painted scars running all the way up to her ankles,

"Car accident" She said

"And the rest of you was untouched…funny…"

"Got $10,000 in insurance when I get back home"

"I don't trust you"

"Why?"

"You're too beautiful"

"Too beautiful my ass…I'm too fat, look at this" She grabs her thigh jiggling it around "I should lose ten pounds"

"Like hell"

"I'm 145 pounds, you know?"

"Rocking good news"

"Ooooh, you like big girls, don't you?"

"To a point, of course…here have some wine"

"Give it here, boy…touch my thighs"

"Oh yeah…"

"Feel how big they are?"

"Sure, yeah, oh yeah…"

"These are thighs, don't you know?"

"I know, I know baby, hammock heaven!"

"You see, these are legs, not that skinny fucking shit you see in Hollywood movies, you know?"

"In full agreement here…"

"Tell me you love big thighs"

"I love big thighs"

"Again"

"Big thighs, ooooohh yeah"

"Not bad for a high school chick, ey man?"

She rubbing her leg gently against me my hand on her ass,

"I don't want to get close to you, Jasmina"

"Why do you say things to purposely hurt me?"

"When do you go back to Strasbourg?"

"July 27"

"That's only 5 months from now"

"Let's have some wine, who gives a shit about tomorrow"

"I agree, fuck it all...just don't expect too much from me"

"Drink your wine, tough guy"

She laid into me softly her sweater taking me in smelt her perfume felt her lips on my cheek we hugged and grinded whispering bullshit to each other,

"I expect nothing" She said sadly,

"Best way to go through life"

"A bit sad, but..."

"Not so sad...it doesn't mean we can't have a good time, you know?"

"Was it Henry Miller that said...how did he say?... 'even if the world is busy flushing itself down the toilet, there's still time to sing and dance'…something like that…"

I started laughing, "Yeah, something like that"

"You're laughing at my accent, aren't you?"

"No, no, well maybe just a little…"

"You…" She punched me in the arm playfully her tiny fist barely making an indent,

"Anyway, I agree with Miller" I said "have you read lots?"

"Oh yeah, 'Paris is like a whore'"

"Is it true?"

"If you see Paris at night, man…I can sort of see what he means, you know?"

"That is one of the few cities of the world that I want to see…mainly because of 'Tropic of Cancer'"

"It's unbelievable, truly"

"Want to smoke a joint?"

"No doubt"

And it continued just like that, talking swearing drinking and smoking, sun up in full force coming through the balcony and the bay windows like the face of God, our faces flushed and temporarily happy sadness washed away with all the other crazy bullshit, slowly the boys started to wake one set of bloodshot eyes after the other blue sky wanting, Woodstock was on the tube and soon Barney lit a joint with his first coffee while Jake took off and Trent joined in the song and dance noticing my hand on Jasmina's leg, big smile from Barney, Trent looking confused,

 "That better not be Styrofoam you're drinking out of buddy" said Barney to Trent,

 "Fuck you 'buddy', this is my place, spare me your bullshit sanctimony"

 Jasmina looked at me rolling her eyes, Santana was up on Woodstock, 'Soul Sacrifice', and we all got into that stoned and tired and hazy and drunk and forgotten and ignored and the hell with the lot of you…

11.

Few days later was writing and drinking feeling pretty high down in that cool dark basement could have stayed there forever man, sun slipping into the room through the blinds in thin streams felt like I didn't need a damn thing in the world as I wrote a few sentences fast as I could letting the words come out of me like a waterfall-sensation, a lubricated onion field, paused and took a small hoot off the pipe feeling like this was paradise, this feeling of almost- nothingness, this feeling that I'd craved for my entire life not knowing it but sensing the pull, I could feel the tragedy I'd suffered through slipping away from me a bit at a time, I laughed out loud facing the bullshit head-on thinking, 'there's nothing to fear', absolutely fuck-all, the worst thing is death and what the hell could there be to fear about that'? Speaking to myself in the dim-morning-failure there was a knock on the door, goddamn! Fucking hell! All things ruined it's war all the fucking time! I made my way to the door up the stairs feeling damn tired suddenly, opened the door and there she was...

She sat cross-legged on my bed her hair large all one length and curly light brown curls just touching her shoulders me eyeballing her plentiful thighs opens her bag pulls out a Mickey of Scotch hallelujahs all around she smiling right into me huge eyes confessing everything,

"Got any pot?" She said,

"Sure"

We got into the pot leaving the booze alone on the dresser with the shadows and us moving into the dead sunlight blowing out clouds of smoke curling up to the ceiling we was slow-dancing to Billie Holliday deep deep blues all around us, nightlife musings in the corridors long and deep, her large breasts rubbing against me, into me, into the overblown sad-world grayness, the tall whiskey-memories, the blues bar Friday night confessions, easy sliding down heart-gone-cold boulevard, life sad and distant but her cheek on mine man, her crotch stroking me gently in the smoke-filled paradise, until the end of the night long long wanton song blasting your brain-dead musings, she giggling under the influence, her hands on my waist, her big feet clumsy and sensual she spinning around giving me soft kisses hands move to my ass world cruel and far-away gladness, us feeling the luck one more time sweet-sugar-moans, one more time in steady rhythm with the universal be-bop,

"How do you feel?" I said,

"Like a rolling stone" She smiled,

"Like this music?"

"Billie Holliday is one of my favorites...my mom got me into her"

Sadness creeping into things always and forever but we were ready for it man, nothing cool and easy running but nothing impossible either as she starts kissing me more intently feeling her tongue slide into mine warm and wet, feeling the warmth of her body pressing me gently then harder my hand moves to her thigh then between her legs I rub softly hearing her moans almost like a soft cry somewhere in the distance she gets louder and I join in we grooving in perfect time sensation, we long lost sisters of mercy, we moving sunlight madness taxi ride to the moon I bite her neck, she moans louder, I bite again feel her nails on my ribs as the music switched to Louis Armstrong's "Ain't Misbehavin", our bodies grinding hard now ain't nothing delicate here our tongues halfway down each other's throats her hand rubbing my cock pushing at my jeans we roll clumsily to the bed she's on top her full bodyweight laying flat on me my tongue is on her nipples, her hand is around my cock, her jeans are coming off...

In her underwear she looking like magic, sat on my bed on her heels big thighs in full display, it was a gift from the gods too drunk to care, an early morning beer buzz, a woman smiling in a smoke-filled room, her stomach with just the slightest of excess skin barely visible over the underwear line what a trip, we had The Smithereens' "Blood And Roses" on the ghetto both of us talking shit and laughing and smoking and drinking she spoke of her home in Strasbourg relating things slowly and softly,

"Can't stand it there"

"What could be so bad?" Me stroking her hair gently,

"Everyone is so fucking close-minded, it's driving me crazy!"

"Man, you know, the image we get of France in North America, or of all of Europe for that matter, is this incredibly progressive, liberal and artistic place to live...it seems strange to hear what you're saying..."

"Well, in idea, in politics, in philosophy Europe is what you just said, and in a lot of places you can actually feel it...but not in fucking Strasbourg, that's for sure...but I find it very liberal here in Canada, in Winnipeg too…the only complaint I have about this city is that the people themselves don't appreciate it, you know?"

"I've noticed"

"All I hear from everyone is that they're going to finish their degree and move somewhere else, everyone here wants to go someplace else, to the U.S. or to Europe or to Alberta, I've never, in all my travels, seen such a thing in any city…why go anywhere, I don't get it, you have this little rock and roll jewel right here, I don't know…"

"It's money, it's always fucking money, people know they can get more money elsewhere so they split…fucking morons"

"Well how much money do you need? It's not just one house anymore, it's one house PLUS twenty thousand dollars in the bank, two cars, vacations in Mexico, whatever happened to being happy that you have ONE house and a fucking job, christ, sometimes I just can't stand people"

"Hear, hear"

"So how the hell does a student afford a house all to himself?"

"It's my mother's house, I'm house-sitting while she's in Italy"

"Yes, but where do you actually live?"

"Right now, right here"

"What are all these papers, your school work?"

"No, I never bring school home with me…I'm a writer, they're short stories, or attempts at such…"

"Really? I write poetry"

"I don't like much poetry"

"None?"

"Well, I like Bukowski and Kerouac, that's about all the poetry for me"

"Ever read any French poets?"

"No, not really interested"

"You have no idea what you're talking about"

"Alright sister"

"Look, I'll introduce you to some French poets and you can introduce me to this Brukowski…"

"That's BU-kowski"

"Whatever chico"

"Chico?"

"Can I read some of your writing?"

"Sure, take that one over there"

"Which one?"

"The one called Observations, over there….right there man, under your nose…"

"Got it…cool…so are you doing alright at University?"

'You mean my grades?"

"Yeah"

"Easy stuff, I'm just bored, it's artistically stifling, nothing creative about it at all"

"Hmmm"

"So no better than high school?"

"Not at all"

"When I get back to France, I'm enrolling in University right away"

"All the power to ya"

"What does that mean?"

"Good for you, I'm encouraging you"

"Sounds like sarcasm to me man"

"It is actually"

'You, grrrrrr…" playfully punching me in the arm, "You drive me crazy"

"That's good, isn't it?"

"So where the hell do you get your money from?"

"Student loan and grants…got just enough to last me the school year"

"Then?"

"I don't know, maybe I'll sell grass, who cares?"

"I love that attitude, really"

Awkward silence…Jasmina started fidgeting both of us uncomfortable for the first time in each other's presence getting that strange electricity shooting across the room me watching her breasts resting nicely inside that tight sky-blue tank-top her legs stretched out in front of her so fucking long her big scarred feet dangling over the edge of the bed I poured two drinks she taking hers quickly large gulp then her five-foot-ten-inch frame moving clumsily and too cute baby doll across the bed over to my music collection her ass facing me black underwear hugging cheeks like soccer balls she had that Negro ass sitting high up and sticking out cannonball-sexy man,

"Ahh, this is a good one" She said,

"The Breeders, I hear ya"

"Wait, maybe this one"

"What was wrong with The Breeders?"

"Okay, The Breeders it is"

And "Last Splash" came on touching us lightly then my hands on her thighs and we grooving in the samba early morning heat in the down and out rock and roll movement sun setting on my desires bodies wrapped around each other her breath so hot on my face legs wrapped tight squeezing my ribs into dust sun looking ugly mind moving sideways keeping it steady bop bop we going bop bop grinding crotches clumsy and confused fingers inside her she arches her back slides down between my legs takes my cock in her mouth the rock and roll silence all around us...

12.

Walking the early summer sidewalks houses on either side of us large elm trees lined up forming a canopy over the street this high school beauty beside me she feeling old and young at the same time, she in tight jeans radio-madness, she in rock and roll lust, we talked about love and hate sun coming through the trees in golden shafts, baby oh oh oh lookit that sunshine moment man, look at the blue and green all around wanna sing till the end of the final night, she smiles quietly bit of sadness showing through bright bright teeth, nice trees she said, yup I said, playfully gave her a poke she returned the favor little girl coming out again she laughed madly electric orange substance abuse man, madly like the hillside crying, like Ray Charles singing, like the atom bomb on your doorstep, like dirty water screaming, like love peaking around the corner, park bench by the kiddie swings we sat and lit up the marijuana smelling sooooo sweet-morning-blue so gladness-mad-boulevard marvel, she got black dress-shoes black laces tied tight bare feet inside hair long and wide and wild curls everywhere and me thinking of how lucky I was for that one moment, that one sad and beautiful moment, me and Jasmina and

Jasmina's shoes, she trips on the sidewalk I start laughing loud and distant gives me dirty look for a second then starts laughing herself, so we held hands and talked and walked she being two inches taller than me legs as long as midnight, eyes so fucking round and huge I was hypnotized man, could have kissed her from head to toe for hours and planned on doing just that as I lit a smoke inhaling deep deep summer blues, things seeming so far away sky red and purple and endless on the Canadian prairies isolation gravy looking like goodbye in the end, in the end always goodbye, that one word final and irrevocable "goodbye", goodbye wavy-gravy, goodbye long choo choo running, goodbye endless blues and winter loneliness, goodbye happy moments in the moonlight, goodbye brown-green eyes laughing sadly, one day always and forever there comes the final hurrah...but not today man, not today as I take her gently by the arm feeling the contours of her ass and the length of those incredible thighs, feeling the electric warmth of her presence all around we cruising down the golden existence of the MOMENT and I say,

Johnny B. Goode baby,

Johnny be good tonight cuz people

they coming for miles around

doo doo be good tonight Johnny,

go Johnny go go go…

13.

Jasmina would stay in Gimli for the week-days and come stay with me from Thursday to Sunday, those days apart feeling like hell man the realization something serious was happening between us cutting me like a switchblade, but on this Monday night Barney says goodnight, goodnight old friend, time to go back to saving the world one beer at a time, we sat inside The Toad In The Hole he talking and smoking John Player Special's like it's the end of all things,

"Off to Brazil this time…"

"Rio?" I said,

"Just outside, don't remember the name of the town…should be pretty wild"

"I'll bet"

"Listen man, I was thinking…"

"Shouldn't do that, it's not good for the brain"

"I can get you on one of the boats with me, you know?"

"What?"

"On one of the Greenpeace boats, you could sail the world man"

"You gotta be kidding?"

"Why not? That's what writers do, they experience, right?"

"I think I have enough clichés in my arsenal, I'll leave that one to you"

"You don't think it would do you good?"

"Not in the slightest…first of all I don't do communal living…I'm not going to spend months on a fucking boat with those pseudo-hippies…I don't like sharing my everyday experiences with anyone, far too private for that"

"Okay, I hear ya"

"Me sailing the world…never heard anything so damn hilarious"

Silence…for awhile…could hear The Replacements in the background, few guys at the bar commenting "sounds like garage rock" one guy says, "more like that alternative shit" says the other, world chockfull of morons, there is a shortage of food, medicine, rain, sun, money money money, love, compassion, understanding, grace and charm, yet never, never a shortage of morons,

"Can't stop thinking about her, you know?"

"Ah the hell with it, she's someone else's problem now" I said smiling,

"Yeah…" he smiled back weakly "You're right…"

"Women, what do they know? Fuck'em"

"All of them"

"Every last one"

"Wouldn't that be nice..."

 "A nice and easy death"

"Well..." Draining his pint "I gotta run"

We hug and he's off, I watched him walk away all dead and beat shoulders hunched head down and I smiled rainbow shivers cuz I knew it was temporary, we were young and nothing could touch us, nothing not permanently, nothing not forever as the moon shines and the booze pours and the laughter runs over the prairies like red red wine on your lonely Sunday suit rainy afternoon away from the world-gone-bloodhungry, world gone white-light white-heat, eyes hungry mad lunatic wanting poor bastard on the corner he got front teeth missing he whiskey-angry he got no love no satisfaction native girl at liquor store sad-sixteen gets her fix for the night running through the jungle with random precision fangs looking for fresh meat Scotch and water in my hand always and forever me runnin' too man, me runnin' blinding light all around she sad-sixteen, me sad-mad-27 never knowing each other, never seeing me like firewhiskey in your backyard smoky room blues band shakes Jasmina's hips "yeah yeah yeah" ain't never too late she got tongue like velvet, legs like mr. tambourine man, she calling me over breasts going jug jug jug, I follow into the blinding light of living through the haze and electric sadness, through the mad grip society, through the endless parade I follow cuz she sweet and lowdown, she slow-mad-sexy, she got red underwear touching my lips in world-gone-dizzy…

Then the fights came of course, wouldn't be human without them both intelligent not all opinions similar and I loved Jasmina's lips as she got angry man they got pouty thick and red, eyes narrowing she sexy jealous beauty fuming mad over ex-girlfriends of mine as I would mention them purposely to see those lips angry, that ass jiggle away from me, those hands waving madness through the air, French accent flying with the insults me giving it right back and suddenly, suddenly, it ends…then we laughing in the sun once again as she told me all about her high school with maturity and deep thought she reflective way beyond her eighteen years leading the way for me to depart on one of my famous diatribes about anything and everything, and her laying on the bed with her head in her hands elbows up feet kicking behind her like a little girl, won't you love me madly? I talked about University and my psychology classes, philosophy, English literature, theology, sociology, art, history, film studies, really dug film studies the rest boring the shit out of me all too easy and structured for a wild-uneasy mind like mine, never liking the world much I was still capable of seeing the beauty in it, never liking people much I was always amazed at how many damn fine individuals I'd met in my life, got along with most people and most people got along with me seeing my easy-going side, my friendly nature, my love for a good time and almighty thirst, my ability to shimmy and shake under most conditions, my brooding side there too but only to those who REALLY knew me, I was introspective with reclusive tendencies the paradox being I LOVED a good time man, loved to rattle and groove all night long with all kinds of people, from small-time criminals to University professors to drug dealers and hookers to blue collar workers and the mighty proletarian to musicians and artists and family men and killers, only to retreat and not want a single soul to invade my space for days on end me and my marijuana-mornings, my trippin' California dreaming, my Sid Vicious nasty, my Tom Waits whiskey afternoons doors and windows shut listening to The Pixies dim room peaceful shadows blue smoke curling to the ceiling world so far away enormous silence singin' like Alex Harvey see you soon blue moon, that nothing-doing nothing-going feeling all around as I gently slide three fingers inside her tongue on her breasts she biting my shoulders wild animal unleashed she moving wild sunshine leather thighs around my neck squeezing till face goes blue man, got the face-gone-blue blues our mouths bashing away then soft kisses early dusk settling in she slides all over me like a jungle-queen man she biting my shoulder ouhgghh jesus man oh man, teeth move to my midsection leaving marks, nails digging into my ribs I grab a handful of her hair and let it rip our bodies grooving in rock and roll sensations sweaty and awkward and digging it we mounting jacks in the cold desert heat, we singing dandelion songs in the winter, we scaling mount Olympus naked and ugly revenge on our minds, we moving like Lightning Hopkins at smoke-filled blues bar, Robert Johnson at the crossroads, we LSD- daydream-believers born to be wise, we Rum and coca-cola wisdom smiling into the abyss, we punk rock violence c'mon baby we singing songs about love and hate as I kissed her gently, twice on the cheek then settled on her lips for a slow long moment, her lips warm and wet we continued like that hearing the rain on the windowsill, slowly at first, then picking up the beat in rhythm with our sad slow-lament beauty…

14.

A kiss to build a dream on…

Sometime in May rainy summer strange thing for Winnipeg where it's always sunny and blue, Jasmina and I on the couch watching the tube an old Star Trek rerun she digging it early afternoon cigarette in hand making circles, she got black underwear bare feet light blue tank-top legs drawn up toes painted deep deep red hatchet murders, now it's true that Romeo loved Juliet and that Lou Reed wrote a great song about it but Jasmina dropped into my life like a gift/curse from the gods man, right at the moment when I was most down and when I desperately needed change but was incapable of making it happen (lack of strength and inspiration) here she comes, here she comes round the mad bad dangerous back alley bullshit smiling and hopeless, I was cooked man, I was trapped INTO Jasmina, I was hers and the thought terrified me cuz in a few short months she would be gone gone gone daddy's gone, goodbye yellow brick road and everything else with it…hated myself for not being capable of simple affair with this woman, just a summer sex-romp in the wild, hated my feelings for showing their fucking face when a good clean simple summer-long fuck would have been the cat's ass man, so we went out that night ran into the gang at The Spectrum and had another wild night of drunken debauchery, of rock and roll visions moonlight just right seeing double of everything cool and wicked, Trent and Jake hitting on the girls Jasmina and I bouncing up and down shots of Sambuca and back alley marijuana jaunts me with my Scotch and water she her Gin and Tonic arm in arm cheek to cheek to the live alternative rock it was Bob's Your Uncle that night, one of the great alternative bands of the time lead singer young and sexy Asian woman doing the alternative jig-jig this band was strange and inventive and exciting to be around, later that evening she and me on the carpet bashing teeth but I was pulling back, I was hesitant, she frowning into my eyes sits up topless breasts bouncing in rhythm to the sadness, blue underwear hugging bowling-ball ass-cheeks, toes painted aquamarine, she looking grim and confused gently rubbing my arm,

"What is it?" She saying,

"Listen, ahh, I think maybe we should call it quits"

"Quits?"

"Yeah"

"Quits, you mean us?" She looking angry,

"Well what else?"

"Oh, and sarcasm too?"

'Look, we've gotten way too close for such a short time, you know?"

"Well what's wrong with that? I mean, what does that tell you, we're supposed to be together, c'mon…"

"Look, you're leaving in…what's the actual date?"

"July 27"

'That's two months from now man….know what I mean?...i mean, I'm sorry but I was just getting over something when I met you…I can't go back to that place again, I won't make it out…"

"Well what happened? Do you feel comfortable telling me, or…?"

"I'd rather not…listen-"

"-look, I know you've been fucked up over women before, what was her name?"

"Fuck her"

"Well…you're the one who's always talking about the MOMENT, live for today, enjoy it while you can, all that stuff…"

"Well-"

"-I mean, aren't you doing the exact opposite?"

'Look, all things being normal, the moment is what I live for, but it's been pretty shitty for awhile, I guess I'm too fucked up right now, I don't know, look WHAT THE FUCK, what do you want from me?"

Jasmina's eyes turning red and smoky she looking angry-sad,

"Well, I'm not going to beg you, that's for sure" She got up started dressing everything blurry and out of control she moving lightning-speed Concrete Blonde's "Happy Birthday" in the background I grab a beer start drinking see Jasmina from the corner of my eye clothes covering her up one piece at a time she stealing glances in my direction see those beautiful legs disappear into tight jeans she stands in corner crosses her arms staring at me feeling that hot glare on my temples drinking beer not returning the glance she storms out the door all the singing gone, misty-morning-blue on the doorstep she whiskey-hungry, madman-hipster he frowning pointing fingers, lonely arcade sits there smiling lights gone out, all the singing gone,

see you lovely, see you blue moon…

15.

So I wandered the streets alone again feeling down but nowhere near defeated, nowhere near and never completely says mooney suzuki drum roll as I walked in and out of bars missing school for a week not giving a damn cuz it's only school, not real at all, an illusion of the mind full of asshole tendencies and virgin suicides says Jennie squeezing tight, found myself in The Osborne Village with the rest of the freaks and fringe-living jackasses, street artist says hello I blow her a kiss moving in steady-slow movement never coming home feel the distorted guitar like a buzzsaw killer words in the sudden mind-melt reality Jesus he there smoking Turkish cigarettes he smiling "go on" he saying "no fear sucker" cobblestone street running away from me Mohawk children asking for change Native guy painting rainbows on the sidewalk me smiling no fear fucker moving slow behind cigarette dangling from rotten lips rocket from the crypt launches slow-mojo-working me slow-joe-deadly feeling mean-trouble- wanting not too tired to rock Jimi slowhand guitar groove cuz nobody knows watch out baby six-string in my hands riffin' electric-glide slip-sliding over the floor Osborne Village

Freaks all around hot Saturday afternoon my mighty thirst in overdrive seeing everything blinding visions fat-girl-lazy she so sexy all day long through the sun beating down on bus-stop-horny sound of girls working the night sweet munki hooker cranks it up gimme juicy afternoons in the air conditioned nightmare she screaming in the city of always-night beep bop bop cocksucker blues raging hard-on wanting wild woman fancy midnight-alley-girl alone in the salty moonlight alto-bass goes dumm-de-doodly-dumm-dong got my shaft rising steadily listless parade right behind me hear the New Orleans jazz Dixietown beauty she got brown legs shaking sexy fat and long cellulite heaven up and over follow me says he long beard flowing, hey, old friend over there Leo goddamn crazy fucker, he young Native artist beautiful acrylic renditions of native philosophy and spirituality he got front teeth missing big gut loud infectious laugh we shake hands under the stars man, we happy trippin' down the sidewalk Leo half-drunk talking to all the girls big smiles chain smoking life one drag at a time, we down the road loving and living stop off at a patio right by the street watching the multi-colored mohawks and the pierced everythings walking right by, guy with purple hair laughing on the corner, lesbians making out under streetlight single car blasts its horn as it goes by, Leo looking tough and hangover as usual t-shirt and jeans black shoes got goatee and tobacco stained fingers, lived the hard streets raised on Native reserve starving artist in the classical sense learned much from Leo and he from me as we shoot back the Sambuca living large he telling me about his latest thing, got young woman barely legal staying with him,

"As long as she's legal" I said,

"Exactly"

"So she's alright?"

"She's an alright chick man, she's allllllllright"
Leo pointing fingers at the sidewalk full of the outside-people, people like us, no-money artists, starving students who don't go to school, down-low-hustlers, dreamers dreaming of other places but diggin' where they are, digging the beautiful women of Winnipeg,

"Why does this fucking city have so many gorgeous fucking women?" Said Leo,

"Don't know man, don't question cuz it's so damn lovely"

"Crazy fucker ha ha ha"

"Here's to Winnipeg girls"

"Winnipeg girls yuk yuk slammer"

He knew nothing of what I'd recently experienced and I wanted to keep it that way, wanted to keep him untainted by my bullshit but I did tell him of Jasmina,

"You're a crazy fucker…it's always the same with you, stay alone for months then all of a sudden you've got this fucking beautiful woman hanging off your arm, then you tell her to fuck off, and you're alone for months again, then it starts all over, what is it with you?"

"Well it's not that fucking laid out man"

"If I were you I'd say FUCK what happens two months from now, get into that chick man, you guys dig each other, don't turn away asshole"

"Check it out"

Beautiful goth lady a heartbeat away very tall maybe 6 feet tattered fishnets hair platinum blonde watch her walk by Leo drooling man-child draining beer after beer so full of life, so full of sadness and laughter, triumph and failure, in his presence you felt electrified, sometimes annoyed cuz he was loud and tough and drunk and fist-fighting no stranger but man, he was alive!

"How's the writing going man?" He said,

"Pretty damn good, I write more than I go to University…don't have the nerve to send it off to publishers yet…"

"What? With all the crap that's out there?"

"Lots of shit out there, I agree…how about your art?"

"Well, creatively couldn't be better…financially, I'm barely scrounging a living…"

'What the hell man, this isn't a society where art is held at high value…design a new type of hair jell and you'll be a millionaire"

"What the fuck, lookit that"

It was there in front of us, all of it, all the meaning and secrets and discovery and purpose and need and beauty and ugly and desire, all that was needed was VISION, maybe a bit of understanding, all that was needed was DO WAH DIDDY DIDDY, MAN ON THE MOON, LAST OF THE TEENAGE IDOLS, it's all here cocksuckers, can't you see it, can't you? We need to sing man, doesn't have to be in unison, doesn't have to be in tune as a matter of fact better if out of tune hippy hippy shake baby to the left and right and all around, we continued as the sun set our asses nailed to those chairs the drinks coming non-stop Leo paying for most and we laugh and laugh cuz with Leo it's love or misery no between-stuff, no way, sing till the end of the rabid laughter you crazy fucker, sing for me and all the rest of us blind and naked motherfuckers, sing all the way down tobacco road, cigarette heaven whiskey triumph she just a touch away…

16.

Night at The Spectrum...with some friends watching a punk band called Honest John And His Merry Men leaning up against the bar tap on my shoulder, Jasmina she standing there furrowed brow looking right into me, we hugged and started laughing no sentimental bullshit just the knowledge that this thing was beyond us, it was going the distance right up until her plane took off into the prairie sky, she motioned me outside and took my hand, me behind watching her ass move inside a pair of blue dress pants her curly thick brown hair moving like an earthquake, whoa, all eyes on her cuz she too gorgeous sugar-sweet, outside two friends young French broads part of her exchange program they both hot and sassy, one with red hair great sense of humor by the name of Chantel she sexy big thighs young woman, she bright and full of the white-light baby, other a short brunette softer and kinder but nice size legs too and sexy-sweet smile, we talk hah hah ahah, ain't it nice ha ha hah, me and Jasmina incapable of keeping our hands off each other,

"Wow" Said Chantel "You guys must be in love"

I flip a cig into my mouth as me and Jasmina move away just slightly,

"Listen" She said "I have to go with them tonight"

"Where you guys going?"

"I think it's called Earl's On Main…"

"Christ, that place fucking sucks, it's all the beautiful people, very upscale"

"I know, I'd rather be with you, but how about tomorrow?"

"Well let me check my calendar…no, of course, I'll see you"

"Can I knock on your door about 3 in the afternoon?"

"You can knock on my door anytime…I'll see you tomorrow"

Our lips met…it was nothing but history from there…

17

Goddamn hot fucking summer afternoon even with the sun behind clouds we was in the backyard laying on the grass after getting high she in a pair of jean cut-offs small and tight without being slutty, me in my jeans and beetle boots as always dressed the same in any season didn't like to expose my body cuz it's my body sweet and lowdown, she barefoot as always loved having her feet kissed said she liked it almost, almost better than anything,

"You know, there is one thing…"

"Yeah, what's that?"

"One thing I like more than anything…"

"Well, sex, right?"

"No, no…I mean I love it, but c'mon, everyone loves sex, have some originality"

"Sometimes I think sex is the most overrated thing in the universe…yet…"

"Well, I'm only 18, it's not like I've had tons of it, but it seems to be the, umm, usually, the same thing over and over, you know?"

"I know, and yet we always think about it, we always want it, I don't know…I'm looking at your legs and I'm thinking-"

"-Hold on, you always go into a million topics at once-"

"Got an intense mind baby, what do you want?"

"There was something I wanted to tell you…show you"

"The one thing you like above all else?"

"Yeah…let's go inside…okay?"

"Alright, rocking good news"

Two or three hours later, sore ribs and chest, stomach not so good either, interesting experience this Jasmina, not so innocent kinky French girl,

"I'm not going to ask you if you're alright because it would ruin the whole idea, you know?" She said,

"I see"

"I'm going to Vancouver with the Exchange Program"

"For how long?"

"A week and a half"

"When?"

"Tomorrow"

"Can you spend the night?"

"No, I wish…gotta go in a couple of hours"

She laid into me head on my shoulder both of us smoking Winston Lights and the soundtrack to Twin

Peaks softly in the background, room dim continual rain outside moving lightly across the rooftop,

"This is beautiful music" She said,

"Know what it is?"

"Yeah, it's that David Lynch show….he's huge in France, I think more respected than he is here"

"You mean more respected than he is in the U.S….we're more appreciative, by and large that is, of art in this country…why do Europeans always combine the U.S. and Canada? We're very different, you know?"

"Well, I've been to both lots of times, I don't see much difference"

"You're crazy, what you see is surface similarities, we are fundamentally two entirely different nations…Canada is more alone, sadder, and therefore more interesting…not to mention one hundred times more liberal and open and artistic"

"I love the way you talk…I really…God, I don't know…when that day comes for me to leave…"

"Hey, were not supposed to talk about it, remember?"

'It's going to be so fucking hard" Her eyes full of tears she fights them back and smiles "One moment at a time, right?"

"Right"

"Do you think life is fair, I don't think life is fair at all, the idea of Karma is bullshit"

"Maybe, maybe not...is it not a good thing that we met?...maybe it's not about how long something lasts, but about how damn fine it is while it lasts..."

"That's an-about-face from what you were saying just last week"

"I woke up"

"Alright...I feel sleepy, how about you? Can we take a nap?"

"Sure...sure..."

And as it goes, we slept...

18.

Jasmina sent me a postcard from Vancouver her and two friends I met laying on the beach side by side in their bathing suits friend Chantel cocking a heavy thigh upwards, Jasmina in a black one-piece looking sexier than when I'd seen her naked long full thighs splayed out on the sand my tired eyes going straight up the inseam and resting in the middle of the magic, in the lion's filthy den there are no survivors but the fearless like myself take no fucking prisoners, then just like that she was back and we spending more and more time drinking like a couple of barflys which we were not, began vomiting at about that time two or three times a day whether I was drinking or not began to get a bit worried first thing in the morning I'd let her rip, then again in the afternoon sometimes at night as well, very very strange for a guy who had always had perfect health,

"Don't worry about it" I told Jasmina,

"I'm going to miss the shit out of you"

Looking into each other feeling the pain caressing her too-sweet face so young and beautiful mysterious kissing trying to forget about tomorrow cuz it's pure nonsense there is NO tomorrow man it's all illusion, it's a dream, it's a rock and roll fallacy, it's a moment in the sunshine, it's tears in the rain, it's hello dolly big tits sensation, her eyes filled up with water but the tears never came cuz she too strong and cuz it was time for laughter and celebration and I finally got her to smile, then she smiled some more, then the laughter came and we opened a few beers smoked a joint watching the constant rain outside the window holding each other listening to New Orleans Jazz just like in the Woody Allen movies clarinet blowing softly snare drum going tap tap tappity tap…

19.

We decided to take a bath together watched the hot water fill the tub as Jasmina took her clothes off perfectly comfortable with her body (those Europeans man!) me taking my clothes off self-consciously found some of that bubble shit bubbles everywhere man got inside held each other sweat trickling down my forehead Jasmina smelling like an early morning in the rain all beauty and wonder, the world should smell like this I thought we started joking around laughing and talking as I sponged her body those long legs seeming to go on forever, those gorgeous legs that in a few weeks would be in someone else's hands,

"Ohhh, I'm going to be really clean, that's it, get those toes…now the legs…I need a shave, don't you think?"

"Let me do it"

"Okay sexy"

Put the razor to her leg moving down the calf so slowly man enjoying every single curve,

"That's funny"

"What do you mean?"

"Here's how I do it…see…very fast, I just want to get it over with"

"Give me that razor back...I'm trying to enjoy it you goof..."

"Ha ha ha...okay okay"

"See, nice and slow, easy man"

"I have nice calves, don't you think?"

"Unbelievable...the nicest legs I've ever seen, no bullshit...and I'm a leg man"

"No doubt...tell me how nice they are"

"Nice nice nice, very round"

"Are they the roundest calves in the world?"

"The roundest"

"Now say it with your eyes closed"

"The greatest calves in the world, but I'm a thigh man"

"Oooohhh...here you missed a spot...right here on the back"

"Can I open my eyes?"

"Go ahead"

"Okay, yeah, I see it...here, shift over...there, I got it...next leg"

"Do this one better...nice and slow..."

"Oh, now you like it slow?"

"C'mon, just do it"

"Alright, close your eyes...hmmmm, all that flesh"

"Ooooh, that feels so good..."

"There you go...done"

"I don't think I've ever had legs this smooth"

"Do you want a drink?"

"Forget the drink for once…here, turn around…let me comb that tangled mess you call hair"

"Fuck that shit"

"C'mon, you have nice hair but the back is tangled up"

"This isn't about nice hair, Jasmina"

"Oh, I forgot, you're a tough guy…c'mon, turn around"

"Alright, alright"

"You're slightly losing it in the back here, you can tell where one day you'll have a bald spot"

"Well ain't that nice…"

"Man, it's really tangled…really long, I wish mine was this long…here we go…where's the conditioner?"

"Fuck the conditioner"

"There it is, hold on…a nice big wad of cream.."

"I'll show you a big wad…"

"Alright tough guy…let me rub it in…see, look how nice it looks…okay, I'm putting the comb through it"

"JESUS…WHAT THE FUCK!"

"Relax, it'll be over in a minute"

"Relax my ass!"

"How the hell did it get so tangled? Here comes the comb again"

"SHIT!"

"See, look how easy the comb goes through"

"BULLSHIT WITH THE EASY! BULLSHIT!"

"Oh…sorry, does it hurt?"

"Sorry like hell, you love this…FUCK ME!"

"Trust me, this hurts me more than it hurts you, heh heh…there, we're making progress"

"LIKE HELL, FUCK PROGRESS, I HATE FUCKING PROGRESS!"

"C'mon, we're almost there, couple more strokes…"

"AHHH, FUCK THAT'S IT, I'M GETTING OUT!"

"Alright you baby…wait…let me get out first"

I slid back my head just above water level as Jasmina stood up placed one foot on my stomach one on my chest standing on me sideways, uggggghhh I exhaled, she leaning from side to side my ribs bending internal organs screaming aaaaaaaaahh toweling herself off taking her time humming a French song dancing on my prone body feeling like chest caving in finally she got off and out of the tub standing in front of the mirror,

"C'mon, hurry up, we've got things to do" She said,

I caught my breath and got out looking at Jasmina's long naked body like a lost highway,

"Here, I've got a pair of scissors, let me trim your beard"

"Not a fucking chance baby"
I threw her my tattered bathrobe she slipping long body into it inch by inch my underwear comes on we walking to my room she grabbed her tank-top throwing it at me,
 "Tie me up with this...do whatever you want to me"
 She opened the robe showed me her tits then she showed me all the rest, I tied her wrists tightly and did exactly what I wanted afternoon moving gently through the purple haze do wah wahh diddy kissing her lips around the ears her nipples round and pink my lips all over them slowly mind-fuck shake once again rain always rain hitting the window stomach churning Jasmina's open body glistening wet and wild she wiggling crazy moonlight serenade whiskey-hungry old soul wanting love luv sadness she moaning purring cluck cluck mouth slightly open tip of tongue between her teeth rainbow purpose mind in full flight man God gone missing he cruising the universal slow-down-moment old witch on neighborhood stoop she smoking pipe tobacco lost on the horizon keyboard solo waxing through the long-lost mad bad road movie, afternoon slowing down slow-easy Jasmina's chest moving in and out, in and out, slower, slower, waves crashing gently on the forlorn bus-stop, then stop...

20

Royal Albert Hotel draft night punkers everywhere a gathering of skinheads and Mohawks the good looking guys with the George Clooney haircuts there as well hated that sandal wearing type 50 cent drafts in big mugs tasting like shit but going down anyway soon we red-eyed, we happy boozehound babies, we swimming with the lepers high on living distant, knew guitar player in band old friend Jasmina knew him too, knew him before she knew me they talked and laughed and hugged and it was good to see them like that good buddies in the smoke-filled moondance reality, he went back on stage and Jasmina began cruising the room talking to everyone seems she knew half the bar all men of course and the ones she knew were the George Clooney haircuts with their sideburns and sandals and predictability and the hell with them good looks and all, I would approach her and she would ignore me time and time again so I straddled the bar and ordered one scotch after another wondering why Jasmina was pulling this high school flirting bullshit, playing games no doubt all women always playing fucking games with me and my tired mind missing gray matter, so she come up to me tall blond stud by her side,

"Hey, this is John, he's in my class"

"Hi" I said,

"He's a good friend of mine" Said Jasmina to John waving a hand in my direction,

"You're a lucky guy" Said John,

"She's a lucky girl" I said, tough and beat and fuck you buddy,

He looking at me, then Jasmina, then walking away afraid and desperate,

"What the fuck's with you? You didn't have to treat him like that"

"He's playing the same fucking game you are Jasmina, that fucking flirting bullshit game"

"You're just jealous"

"Yes, congratulations, you've succeeded"

"Fuck you"

"Right back at you…this is the first fucking time I've seen you act your age"

'And this is the first time I've seen you act like a tough guy, mr. macho"

"Now how the fuck would you react to me introducing you as 'my good friend'? Do all your 'good friends' chew on your nipples?"

"Well what was I supposed to say? I'm gone in three weeks…I…"

Silence…the band was covering "I fought the law", The Clash version…silence…

"I'm taking off" I said,

"Well what the fuck, I'm coming with you"

"You don't have to"

"C'mon, don't be ridiculous, of course I'm coming"

"Let's get the fuck out of here"

Bought some beer cab-ride home silent watching the rain on the window blurring my view of the streets feeling sleepy and alone and mighty angry…

That night we lied in bed in silence listening to Concrete Blonde's "Bloodletting", me sipping on Scotch she curled up against the wall her back to me a foot of space between us everything dead and silent and distant, touch of moonlight coming through the blinds in slivers my dream lover gone liquor down my throat burning all the way my mind moving in many directions at once wondering why the hell and what the fuck, finished the Scotch started on the beer Jasmina awake but not moving bad electricity running through the room felt its bite up and down my body thinking of years ago when I played guitar in a rock band feeling so fucking free man, not a single care or worry didn't give a damn about anything just wanted to get up on stage and let it fucking fly, tell me your name baby, shout it just right like a whisper in the fog luv luv luv that creamy you, Jasmina stirred then turned and faced me still curled up like a ball her hand caressing my arm she started talking sleepy voice deep and sad,

"I kinda slept...but not really, it was strange, it was like half-sleep, you know?"

"Yeah, I do it all the time...how do you feel?"

"I'm sorry about tonight...at the bar"

"Forget it, it was nothing"

'No, you were right, I was flirting to get you jealous...it was stupid, infantile..."

"Don't worry about it..."

She moved closer her body pushing into me soft moans echoing in the sad mad world I felt the tears on her eyes and held her close, her arms around me she so brave tears rolling down her cheeks slowly she does nothing to hide them but she dignified proud face passive so there we were, two lost lovers rolling down the river standing on street corner watching the hookers eating snails and mustard junky mind-groove waving goodbye she gone daddy, she gone...

We sat in a small park under the canopy of trees that covered most of the city goddamn beautiful in summer enough green to strangle the shit out of you, mosquitoes hovering but no big deal when you're counting the minutes baby, couple of squirrels chased each other up a tree, few birds sang out-fucking-loud overhead, Jasmina in her usual jean-shorts and bare feet tank-top hair running wild in the prairie wind sandals in her hand as she talked and talked and talked we feeling alright me listening cuz she so sweet-wonder-girl, she so tender-lips-wanting,

"Listen, I, ahhh…"

"What's up, Jasmina?"

"I want to talk to you"

"Alright shoot, you crazy rock and roll chick"

"C'mon, I'm serious…put that stick down, what are you doing playing in the mud?"

"Sorry, what's up?"

"You're such an infantile"

"That's what you love baby, ain't it so?"

"Listen, I was thinking…"

"Shouldn't do that, it's bad for the brains"

"Jesus, I could kill you at times…listen, uhmm, what would it take to move to Canada?"

"What? I don't know, I mean, shit…"

"Well I would have to speak to the Canadian Embassy back home, you know, thousands of people immigrate every single year from Europe to North America, there are ways"

"Ummm, what are you saying?…exactly…"

"Alright, if I told you I would move back to Canada next year, what would you say?"

"I would say, rocking good news!"

"I mean, I would be moving back for you, are you getting this?"

"Man, are you kidding me, of course I would dig it…but…"

"You know, we could get married – "

"-What?"

"Bear with me, get married just so I could stay here…a friend of mine moved to the U.S. last year and that's what she did…it's the only foolproof way of doing it, the government can't say shit if you're married"

"Well, I – "

"-I know you don't believe in marriage, neither do I, we would get divorced after the allotted time, you know?...just so I can legally stay here...so we can try our luck, you know, me and you?"

"I would do it without hesitation Jasmina, for you and only you..."

Silence...

"Do you think we can do it?" I said "I mean, long-distance relationships, they kinda suck, I don't know if it's possible...it would be a full year..."

"Nothing happens in a year...I think we can try...at least we can try..."

"Alright, let's see what happens when you go back to France, I'm open...I mean..."

She looking sad suddenly,

"Alright you crazy rock and roll chick, let's go for a walk, maybe a drink or two, I feel like going downtown, c'mon woman, let's hit the road baby!"

"Lead the way mister"

Rain just finished we walking down Broadway in downtown Winnipeg sun peaking it's head round the corner we passing hot-dog stands smelling the burnt carcass delicious baby wandering holding hands in the final minutes before def-con 12 her big thighs young and strong just the right amount of jiggle she looking into my weary eyes getting buzz-light sensation hang on tight we laughing and talking and wondering and dancing and singing and feeling low and feeling happy and hanging on to something very real we hooked into each other and it's okay cuz all things, all things must keep moving, no way around it, sun out now baby beating heavily on my head have always preferred the rain but Jasmina man, Jasmina like a kid in the middle of perfect discovery, she talking loud and laughing energy shooting across the downtown streets right upside your head, we entered a mall right on the main artery fucking cars zooming by electric orange acid trip in youth-land, she shopping for shoes me watching those big scarred feet beautiful and tasty slipping into one shoe after the other then giving up, FUCK IT she said, find a bookstore down the hall she suggesting we buy each other a book very romantic young kid I buy her "Notes Of A Dirty Old Man" by Charles Bukowski, she buys me "Illuminations" by Rimbaud leaving the store and in no time on a bus and in the Osborne Village again, find a bar relatively cheap booze we sitting on barstools Jasmina's fleshy thighs spreading out on the seat she orders coffee Rye and 7 for me,

"Love this neighborhood, almost looks like certain parts of Europe...not quite, but almost... I worry about you throwing up all the time, any ideas?"

"Fuck it, not important, too young to worry about that shit"

"Hope you're right…what a nice day, lookit the wet streets and the sun, I think it's symbolic, don't you?"

"It's a nice thought, let's get drunk"

"Have you ever thought that you might like living in Europe?"

"I'm from Europe, I was born in Italy, went to school there, remember?"

"I mean as an adult"

"Maybe I would, but you know better than to say that to me, I've tried my entire life to not want what I don't have, it's the only way I want to live, I don't care what happens elsewhere, ya dig?"

"I know, I know, just talking…I like all the people in strange clothes around here, lookit that!"

"Whoooweee, far out!"

"God, I can't even think of going back to fucking France"

"Is it that bad really?"

'Well, not France as a country, but my corner of it sucks"

"Really?"

"After a year here, after meeting you, the idea of trying to talk to those idiots I used to call my friends drives me fucking crazy man, fucking crazy...I don't want to go..."

We just kind of looked around feeling the inevitable separation people in the bar laughing ice cubes in the bottom of my drink going tink tink, waiter screaming some shit at someone, door opening and closing, couple in corner under the light arguing about something ridiculous, Jasmina brilliant eyes scanning the place she rubbing her forehead feeling sad and happy and lost and triumphant,

"Let's go home" She said,

"I hear ya baby, I hear ya..."

That night at my place we watched The Rocky Horror movie Jasmina prancing around the room imitating Tin Curry we getting sexual ambiguous wild and fucking horny singing the songs loudly listening to the rock and roll we smooth kissing underwear lonely, lost night fireworks across the sky, she's got my cock deep in her mouth, I'm licking her tits like ice-cream wonder, me rubbing her crotch she moaning moan moan her thighs all over me we sweating clumsy, we sweating like sunshine, we purring like tom-cat-alley, she ties me up and goes wild-honey-wild, got rope burns on my wrists, she got my teeth marks on her thighs, ten thousand cigarettes in the dim late-night-room-lightning, we drunk and tired and maybe even happy, feel the brain going fuzzy, and beyond all odds, all things expected, we sleep…

22.

Last day….we rose with the sun…first thing I saw was her smile that I had to come to know so well in such short time we kissing pretending this day like any other day she speaking my eyes roaming her body resting on her legs jean-shorts as always we kissing sadness suddenly right beside us but we pretend again cuz it's the only way to get through this final escape, we laugh we sing we wonder, she so young, she so beautiful, minutes tick toc tick toc reality hitting home sadness increases with the passing of time we're listening to Mazzy Star, all anger gone, all doubt gone, this moment clear and definable,

"Not going to the airport" I said,

"I know" She said,

Her suitcases in corner we take them hop on a bus walking past the green goddamn fucking green trees all over the place all around all there just for us bus gets downtown in no time we off now, we look at each other we smile man, we smile sad and weak and knowing, bus-stop off the main road once again we under the trees and the caterpillars and the mosquitoes and the ever-lasting shade, we dancing cuz we met in cruel world cruel real-time dizzy man, cuz we know each other forever now, cuz nothing can eliminate this moment, nothing baby, see her bus pull up, we hug and kiss for the last time, her eyes fill up with water, mine as well, goodbye my sweet lovely, see her get on the bus exhaust fumes all around me, started walking aimlessly downtown streets looking nasty as always don't you know baby? Don't you know the messed-up street parade? Followed the beat in certain direction past the Native thugs, the Filipino drug dealers, the white drug addicts, the blacks, the Asians all the peoples, the lost, the workers, the dishwashing wanderers, the security guard slow song lament, hookers hanging on corners looking beautiful and sad, sunny day on the outskirts of meaning, love hidden in the shadows, brown-green eyes gone far far away watch a plane beautiful upward curve disappear into the bright blue prairie sky, trio of drunks carry beer empties to corner vendor they laughing their heads off cuz the happy, couple of cats in a back alley bar-fight see the blood on the pavement, neon sign right in front of me, hadn't seen it in 5 months, The Brass Rail, door closed behind me, scarred faces were just as I left them, couple of tattooed idiots argued over a pool game, hooker on a stool with black eye and thigh-high leather boots, drug dealers out in the open wearing bandannas and expensive clothes, years of alcohol etched in every single face in thick red lines, I took a few steps down, sat on a stool, bartender approaching me,

"Nice to see you make it back, Tony…Scotch and water?"

"No, Rye and 7"

I paid for the drink and started laughing man, had to laugh, there was nothing else I could do…

Tony Nesca was born in Torino, Italy in 1965 and moved to Canada at the age of three. He was raised in Winnipeg but relocated back to Italy several times until finally settling in Winnipeg in 1980. He taught himself how to play guitar and formed an original rock band playing the local bars for several years. At the age of twenty-seven he traded his guitar for a Commodore 64 and started writing seriously. He has published six chapbooks of stories and poems (which he used to sell straight out of his knapsack at local dives and bookstores), six novels, four books of poetry, one short story collection, and has been an active contributor to the underground lit scene for fifteen years, being published in innumerable magazines both online and in print. He currently resides in Winnipeg.

Screamin' Skull Press

Cutting Edge
Spontaneous
Street-Writing

Novels, Stories, Poems

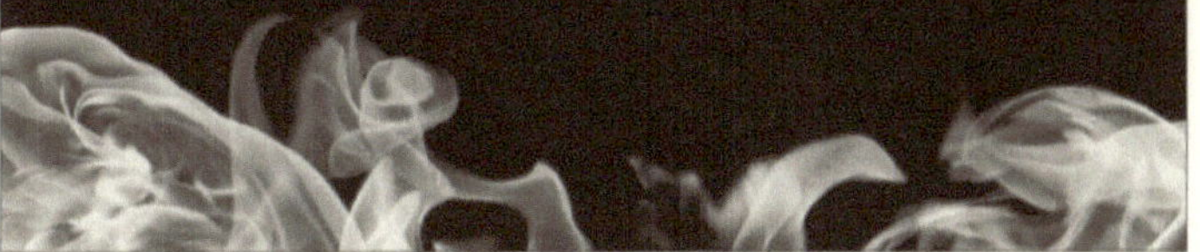

Tony Nesca   Nicole I. Nesca